BRIGHT EYES, BROWN SKIN

WITHDRAWN

BRIGHT EYES, BROWN SKIN

By Cheryl Willis Hudson & Bernette G. Ford

Illustrated by George Ford

SCHOLASTIC INC.
New York Toronto London Auckland Sydney

ISBN 0-590-45416-1

Text copyright © 1990 by Cheryl Willis Hudson and Bernette G. Ford. Adapted from the original poem, *Bright Eyes, Brown Skin,* copyright © 1979 by Cheryl Willis Hudson. Illustrations copyright © 1990 by George Ford. All rights reserved. Published by Scholastic Inc., 730 Broadway, New York, NY 10003, by arrangement with JUST US BOOKS, INC.

32 31   6 /0

Printed in the U.S.A.   23

First Scholastic printing, February 1992

Bright eyes,
Brown skin . . .

A heart-shaped face,

A dimpled chin.

Bright eyes,

Cheeks that glow . . .

Chubby fingers,

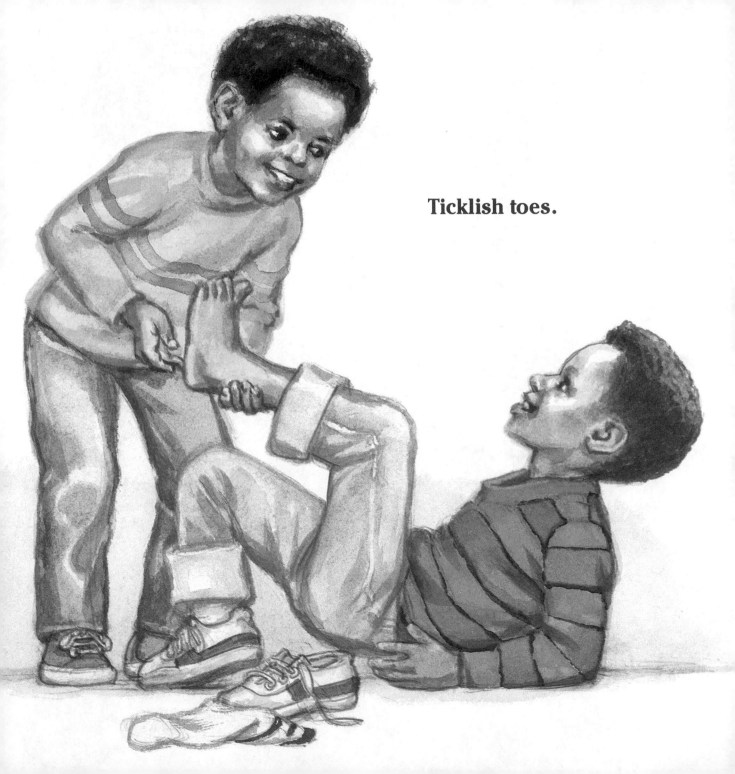

Ticklish toes.

A playful grin,

A perfect nose . . .

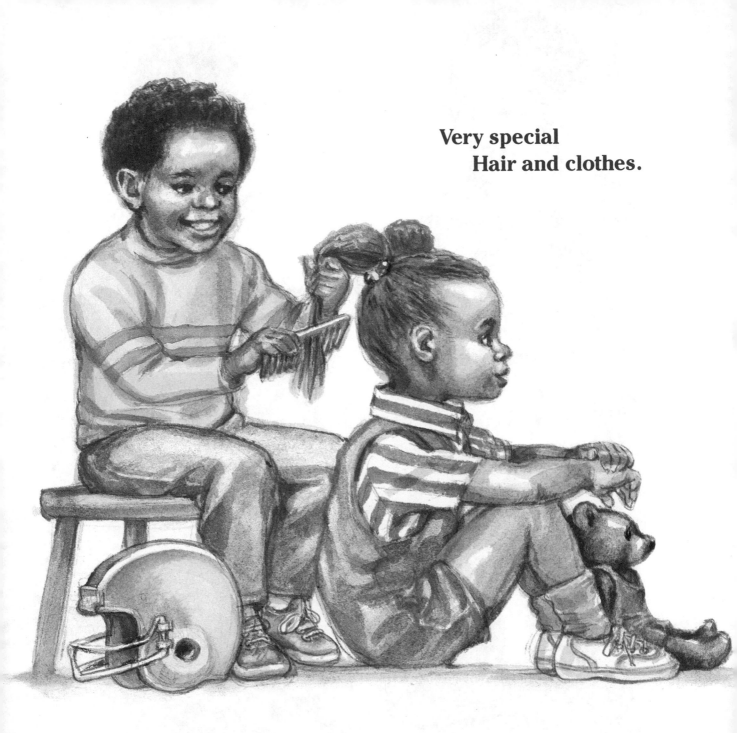

Very special
Hair and clothes.

Bright eyes,

Ears to listen . . .

Lips to kiss you,

Teeth that glisten.

Bright eyes . . .

Brown skin . . .

Warm as toast,

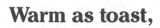

And all tucked in.

Olivia

Jordan

Ethan

Alexa

CHERYL WILLIS HUDSON is an author and graphic designer of children's books. *Afro-Bets® A B C Book* and *Afro-Bets® 1 2 3 Book* were her first published titles, and her poems, stories, and illustrations for children have appeared in *Ebony Jr!* and *Wee Wisdom* magazine. She has designed many books for major publishing companies, as well.

Ms. Hudson, a native of Portsmouth, Virginia, graduated from Oberlin College in Ohio. She now makes her home in New Jersey with her husband, Wade, and two children, Katura and Stephan.

BERNETTE G. FORD is an executive at a major New York City children's book publisher. Under a pseudonym she has written several books for young readers during the course of her career as an editor. Ms. Ford grew up in Uniondale, New York, and graduated from Connecticut College for Women.

This is the first book on which she and her husband, George, have collaborated, but it is not the first time their daughter, Olivia, has appeared in George's pictures. Ms. Ford, George, and Olivia live in Brooklyn, New York.

GEORGE FORD is a distinguished artist who has illustrated more than two dozen books for young readers. He grew up in the Brownsville and Bedford-Stuyvesant sections of Brooklyn and spent some of his early years on the West Indian island of Barbados. Among the books Mr. Ford has illustrated are *Afro-Bets® First Book About Africa, Muhammad Ali, Far Eastern Beginnings, Paul Robeson, Ego Tripping*, and *Ray Charles,* for which he won the American Library Association's Coretta Scott King Award.